THE
TOTALLY NINJA
RACCOONS
AND THE
CATMAS CAPER

by Kevin Coolidge

Illustrated by Jubal Lee

The Totally Ninja Raccoons Are:

Rascal:
He's the shortest brother and loves doughnuts. He's great with his paws and makes really cool gadgets. He's a little goofy and loves both his brothers, even when they pick on him, but maybe not right then.

Bandit:
He's the oldest brother. He's tall and lean. He's super smart and loves to read. He leads the Totally Ninja Raccoons, but he couldn't do it by himself.

Kevin:
He may be the middle brother, but he refuses to be stuck in the middle. He has the moves and the street smarts that the Totally Ninja Raccoons are going to need, even if it does sometimes get them into trouble as well as out of trouble.

CONTENTS

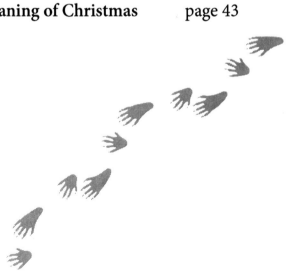

"But you can't just get rid of Christmas!" yelps Huck

1

WHAT'S A KRAMPUS?

It's a cold, blustery winter day outside, but in the super-secret location of the nefarious Cat Board, it is warm and toasty. Hey, just because you are evil and plan on taking over the world doesn't mean you can't be comfortable.

A rather plump, calico cat named Gypsy sits at the head of the table. She does not look merry. Actually, it is safe to say she looks grumpy.

"Uggh, Christmas!" spits Gypsy.

A small, black and white cat wearing a Santa cap tilted to one side perks up. It's Huck!

"The lights, the tinsel, a tree in the house. I love Christmas!" chirps Huck excitedly with a gleam in his eye.

1

A sleek, black cat flicks his whiskers and looks disdainfully at Huck. It's Finn!

"The Twelve Days of Christmas? Absurd! I love Halloween, and Halloween deserves more than just one day. Halloween should be the entire month of October. Black cats are the best. Black cats rule!" declares Finn.

"No, I am the Supreme Head of the Cat Board, and I rule!" meows Gypsy. She clears her throat and adds, "With the guidance of my fellow cats, of course."

A slim tuxedo cat named Velvet speaks up, "The Totally Ninja Raccoons with their black masks would love Halloween to be an entire month."

"Blah humbug, to Christmas: children smile, the humans are happy, they play the same songs repeatedly. I loathe Christmas and I hate the Ninja Raccoons!" growls Gypsy.

A sleek Siamese cat softly purrs and speaks, "Purr-haps we should eliminate Christmas, AND the Ninja Raccoons!"

"Exactly, then there would be more room for Halloween!" shouts Finn.

"But you can't just get rid of Christmas!" yelps Huck.

"Yes, I can! I'll erase Christmas, and replace it with Catmas," proclaims Gypsy.

"But, but, what about Christmas trees?" asks Huck.

"They will be called Catmas trees, and they will contain twice the glass bulbs and catnip toys, but no lights. Those lights hurt my eyes and disturb my naps," complains Gypsy.

"What about presents?" demands Finn.

"All the boxes will be empty!" beams Gypsy.

"Ohhh, empty boxes! Purrre genius, Gypsy. We love empty boxes!" meow all the cats.

"Exactly! And humans who don't already have cats will receive one for Catmas. We will get our fellow felines out of animal shelters, into good homes, and into positions of power," explains Gypsy.

A nearly hairless cat meows. It's one of those Egyptian breed of cats called a sphinx, "Puuuuurrfect!"

"But how are we going to stop Christmas?" asks Velvet.

"Simple, we stop it at the source," declares the Siamese cat.

"Santa Claws! We replace Santa Claws with my substitute Sandy Claws!" yowls Gypsy.

"Who is this Sandy Claws you speak of?" asks Finn.

"I just came up with the name. It's quite clever, don't you think? Sandy Claws is the name I--I mean, we'll give to the replacement for Santa Claus. He'll do our dirty work," says Gypsy.

"Who, or what, are we going to get to do that?" questions the sphinx.

A fat, fluffy Persian cat yawns, "This all sounds like a lot of work. I think I'm going to need a snack and a nap just hearing about it."

"I'll do it! I want to drive the sleigh!" exclaims Huck.

"I should do it. I'm black as night, and I can eat all the tuna from the human's kitchen," meows Finn.

"Nooooo, tuna makes you fart!" yowls Huck.

"Everything makes Finn fart, peee-yew!" meows Velvet as she waves her paws around.

"No, no, no! We need someone with experience. Someone who hates Christmas as much as we do," meows the Siamese.

"I love Christmas!" shouts Huck.

"We need the best of the worst. We need Santa's evil twin. We need Krampus," declares Gypsy.

"Krampus? What's a Krampus?" demand the members of Cat Board.

"Are you going to put that book down and help us get ready for Christmas?" asks Kevin

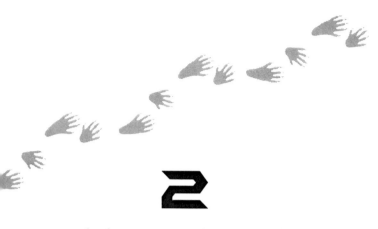

2

CHRISTMAS IS COMING

A white blanket of snow covers the junkyard, making strange shapes out of old cars, and piles of tires, and heaps of trash. A chunky snowman with a tail and cat ears sits on a runner sled next to a little clubhouse. The snowman is wearing a Santa's hat. Inside we hear singing.

He's making a list,
Checking it twice,
Gonna find out who's naughty or nice.
Santa Claus is coming to town!

The Ninja Raccoons work around the clubhouse. Rascal tries to untangle a huge ball of Christmas lights. Kevin unpacks Christmas decorations and Bandit sits on his bed reading a book.

"Are you going to put that book down and help us get ready for Christmas?" asks Kevin.

"I'm reading up on Christmas traditions from around the world," responds Bandit.

"It looks like you are being a scrooge," mumbles Kevin.

"If we lived in Iceland, we could receive a visit from a creature known as the *Yule Cat*," lectures Bandit.

"No, thanks, the Cat Board and Gypsy are enough to deal with," shudders Rascal.

"And if someone didn't do all his chores, the Yule Cat would eat him," announces Bandit.

"Ha, Gypsy will eat **you** if you don't put that book down and help us," says Kevin.

"I think Gypsy may have already eaten some bad girls and boys in Wellsboro," says Rascal.

"Iceland also has a holiday tradition called *The Christmas Book Flood*," reports Bandit.

"Christmas is a bad time for a flood. All that water would turn to ice," says Kevin.

"We could go ice skating!" squeaks Rascal.

"No, Iceland publishes most of the new books around Christmas, and everyone gets a new book on

Christmas Eve. They then go to bed to read and eat chocolate," reports Bandit.

"Ha, Rascal eats chocolate in bed every night. I can tell by all the candy bar wrappers under his bed," announces Kevin.

"I'm storing fat for when I hibernate," explains Rascal.

"Raccoons don't hibernate, but often store fat for the cold winter months. Some mammals sleep more this time of year, but we are ninjas," says Bandit.

"I vote for sleeping more." says Kevin.

"No, we might sleep right through Christmas morning and miss Santa's visit," says Rascal.

"Santa isn't going to bring you anything if you are naughty and don't pick up after yourself," says Kevin.

"In the alpine countries, like Switzerland, there's a creature that will carry you away in a wicker basket if you are a naughty child," states Bandit.

"That doesn't sound so bad. I have short legs, and I get tired walking sometimes," remarks Rascal.

"He carries you away into the wilds, and nobody knows what happens, because you are never seen again," warns Bandit.

"That part doesn't sound so good," shivers Rascal.

"The creature has one cloven hoof, one human foot, horns, and hair all over. His name is Krampus, and he's sometimes called the Christmas Devil," says Bandit.

"Must be hard buying sneakers," quips Kevin.

"I could totally design him a special sneaker," says Rascal.

"Hmmmpf, Krampus is just make-believe. He's something to scare little boys and girls into being good," remarks Kevin.

"The book says that he whips bad children with a switch made of birch," says Bandit.

"Ohh. birch! I love birch beer!" shouts Rascal.

"We know!" reply Kevin and Bandit together.

Bandit closes his book and puts it away on the shelf.

"We don't have to worry about Christmas Cats, Krampus, or Gypsy," says Bandit.

Kevin proudly says, "Yeah, we could take them all anyway, because we are..."

"The Totally Ninja Raccoons!" shout Kevin and Bandit.

"Uhh, a little help here, guys. My paws are totally stuck in these Christmas lights," pleads Rascal.

"Please, just call me Mr. K. I'm working on my image,"
insists Krampus

3

GYPSY MEETS WITH MR. K

It's dark. It's secret. It's Gypsy's secret lair. She's sitting on her big desk with the big, red button in front of her. She still hasn't gotten it fixed, but it matches her new collar.

Gypsy is talking to a creature all covered in fur. He has one cloven foot, horns, and a long tail that waves through the air behind him. He's wearing a bright, green sneaker on his human foot.

"Sooooo, Krampus, I'm looking for someone to replace Santa Claus, aaaand get rid of the Totally Ninja Raccoons. Are you interested?" asks Gypsy.

"Please, just call me Mr. K. I'm working on my image," insists Krampus.

"Exactly, or should I say ex-cat-ly? It's time to bring Christmas in line with the image of the Cat Board. Do you have what it takes, Mr. K?" challenges Gypsy.

"What's in it for me?" demands Krampus.

13

"You could be famous, like Santa Claus. Your name isn't exactly that well-known," says Gypsy.

"I'm pretty famous on the Internet, and popular in Europe," pouts Krampus.

"Don't get me wrong; I love your style. You're wonderful, carting children away with that impish smile of yours. Isn't it time you got what you deserved?" insists Gypsy.

"Well, working just one day a year sounds great, and I could really use an image update, and maybe dental and a new boot," replies Krampus.

"What! Dental with all those candy canes? You'll have a mouthful of cavities in a month. You're killing me." complains Gypsy.

"Ahh, there's no room for sugar in Catmas. Cats aren't able to taste sweet. You cats don't have the taste buds for it," remarks Krampus.

"Wonderful, Catmas is yours, Mr. K! Now, how are you going to break the news to that jolly old elf, Santa Claus?" demands Gypsy.

"I prefer to think ahead. To be pro-active, if you will," replies Krampus.

Krampus claps his hands and five elves dressed in green pull in Santa Claus, tied up with ribbons and a big bow on his head. Krampus takes off Santa's Christmas hat.

"For you, Gypsy," announces Krampus as he places the hat on Gypsy's head. The hat immediately flops over to the side.

Gypsy directs the elves to place Santa into the big, iron cage in the corner.

"Thank mew. How did you manage to capture Santa Claus?" asks Gypsy.

"The elves did it for me. All I had to do was introduce them to the idea of a coffee break," says Krampus.

"That's it? Coffee?" asks Gypsy.

"Yup, and now they are even more efficient. Things are going to get done, and fast," announces Krampus.

"I had coffee once. Terrible, I was only able to sleep fifteen hours that day. Anyway, the North Pole is under control of the Cat Board. Now, just take care of those meddling Ninja Raccoons and world domination is within my grasp," yowls Gypsy.

"You bet, boss. Today the North Pole, tomorrow the South Pole and everything in between," says Krampus.

"Gypsy begins to sing, "I'm dreaming of a white Catmas..."

Santa mumbles, because he can't speak clearly with green duct tape over his mouth. He looks like he wishes he could put his hands over his ears.

"It's even worse than that! Gypsy the Cat is going to take over Christmas and call it Catmas!" says Bigfoot

4

CHRISTMAS TREE, OH CHRISTMAS TREE

It's a snowy winter evening. The ninja raccoons are out in the woods, trudging through the deep snow. Kevin is carrying a saw. Bandit is scouting for a Christmas tree, and Rascal is singing.

"I'm dreaming of a white Christmas. Just like the one I used to snow," sings Rascal.

"It's suppose to go 'Just like the one I used to know," complains Kevin.

"But how is it going to be a white Christmas if it doesn't snow?" asks Rascal.

"That looks like the perfect tree for our clubhouse," says Bandit.

"I'll cut it down, but I'm not carrying it all the way back," says Kevin.

A deep voice comes from out of the darkness, "My cousin can carry it back. He's big and strong," booms the voice.

"Hello, Bigfoot. I didn't see you and your cousin, the Yeti, there," says Bandit.

A huge, white shape steps out from behind the tree, "Well, I am all white. I blend in well on a snowy night, and I'm always dreaming of a white Christmas, too," says the Yeti.

"I can't wait to get this tree back to the clubhouse and decorate it. I've been saving popcorn all year!" squeaks Rascal.

"Uh, I ate the popcorn," says Kevin.

"According to my book, *Christmas Customs from Around the World*, the custom of Christmas trees started right here in Pennsylvania. The tradition was brought over from Germany by immigrants. It was thought to be pretty strange at first, but people enjoyed it, and soon it got popular and the idea spread," explains Bandit.

"A tree inside? What's not to like?" says Kevin.

"Exactly, Christmas trees are evergreen trees, and stay green even in winter. They symbolized to ancient people--such as the Norse--that spring would return and soon green plants would grow again," says Bandit.

"Norse? Those are Vikings! I should have brought an ax instead of a saw," says Kevin.

"I like hanging Christmas bulbs on the branches, as well as the lights, tinsel, and popcorn...if we had any. I'm going to have to use my saved fortune cookies now," complains Rascal.

"Remember, the lights go on first, and about those fortune cookies...." says Kevin.

"It's a beautiful tree, Ninja Raccoons, but it may be the last Christmas tree you'll ever have," says Bigfoot.

"Oh, we always have a real Christmas tree. I love the smell of a tree. It's like having the outside, inside," says Bandit.

"That's not what Bigfoot means. I came to Tioga County to warn my cousin that Santa Claus has disappeared from the North Pole, and if he's not found, Christmas may be canceled," says Yeti.

"But, but, I love Christmas," says Rascal.

"Does that mean I get to sleep in the morning of December 25th?" asks Kevin.

"We have to look into this," says Bandit.

"I told my cousin the Ninja Raccoons would do something about it," says Bigfoot.

"Totally," says Bandit as he puts his paws on his hips.

"Be careful. There are rumors the Christmas Cat is behind this. The Christmas Cat eats children, and probably raccoons too," says Yeti.

Kevin does a big stretch and yawns, "It's probably just Gypsy, the cat, waddling around in the snow."

"It's even worse than that! Gypsy the Cat is going to take over Christmas and call it Catmas!" says Bigfoot.

"Don't be silly. Gypsy couldn't stay awake all night to deliver baseball bats," laughs Kevin.

"Or chocolate!" shouts Rascal.

"Or books!" shouts Bandit.

"I suspect the Christmas Devil, Krampus, is involved. He's usually seen in Germany the night before Saint Nicholas Day, but that's earlier in December, and this year he wasn't seen at all," says Bigfoot.

"Krampus isn't real," says Kevin.

"It's very odd, and I'm worried," says Yeti.

"Not to worry, the Ninja Raccoons will look into it.

Now, let's get this tree back to the clubhouse," says Bandit.

"And cover it in tinsel!" shouts Rascal.

"And Christmas bulbs! Christmas bulbs used to be made right here in Wellsboro when there was a glass factory," says Bandit.

"The shining lights are the most important, and they come first," says Kevin.

"I still haven't been able to untangle the string from last year," says Rascal.

The Ninja Raccoons, Bigfoot, and his cousin Yeti all start hiking back to the clubhouse.

Kevin begins singing, *"Jingle bells, Finn smells, Gypsy laid an egg. The wheels fell off the Catmobile, and Krampus got away..."*

"That's not how Jingle Bells goes," complains Rascal.

No one seems to hear him, and they continue the long walk back to Wellsboro and the clubhouse.

"Hey, wait up everyone! I have little legs!" shouts Rascal.

*Rascal opens both his eyes and yells, "It's Krampus!
It's the Christmas Devil! I told you he was real!"*

5

SLEIGH BELLS

The Ninja Raccoons put up the tree in the clubhouse. It's big and bushy and reaches all the way to the ceiling.

"I'm short. How am I going to put the hubcap star on top?" asks Rascal.

The carburetor angel goes on top this year. Besides, the lights need to go on first. The tree topper is the very last," says Kevin.

"We will get the tree topper on with ninja-style teamwork. We'll do a raccoon ninja pyramid," says Bandit.

"Rascal still hasn't gotten the lights untangled," says Kevin.

"The lights are in a knot. We should just go ahead and decorate the tree," says Rascal.

"It's not a Christmas tree without lights!" shouts Kevin.

"Quiet, you two! It's Christmas Eve, and Santa will be here soon," says Bandit.

"Or Krampus!" yelps Rascal.

"Krampus isn't real," replies Kevin.

"He probably isn't, but we should prepare if he is. Don't worry about unraveling that big ball of lights," says Bandit.

"It's not a Christmas tree without lights!" exclaims Kevin.

"We'll leave a little surprise for whoever visits tonight. If it's Santa, we'll let him go, and if it's Krampus...," says Bandit.

Rascal is stuffing Christmas cookies into his face. His paws and whiskers are covered with powdered sugar.

"Does that mean we don't have to leave milk and cookies out for Santa?" mumbles Rascal through a mouth full of cookies.

"If we don't leave any milk and cookies, we don't get any presents!" shouts Kevin.

"We could leave him some General Tso's chicken and an ice cold birch beer, maybe?" says Rascal.

"Yes, that's a good idea. Santa will probably be hungry, or Krampus," says Bandit.

"Krampus isn't real," says Kevin.

"It's Christmas, and it's the thought that counts," says Rascal.

"I'm sure Santa or Krampus will be just fine with General Tso's chicken and a cold birch beer," replies Bandit.

"Maybe we should leave out a little pork-fried rice too," says Kevin.

"Uhhh, I ate all the pork out of it," says Rascal.

"Let's just finish decorating the tree and go to bed," says Bandit.

"But not to sleep. We have to be ready in case it's Krampus that visits," says Rascal.

"Well, I'm tired. Wake me up for breakfast and presents, but not too early," says Kevin.

"If we don't go to sleep, Rascal, Santa won't land his sleigh," says Bandit.

"What if it's Krampus?" asks Rascal.

"Then I'm eating the General Tso's chicken," says Kevin.

"Maybe I shouldn't leave out a birch beer?" says Rascal.

"Go to sleep, Rascal," says Kevin.

The Ninja Raccoons get ready for bed. Kevin lies down in his hammock and is soon fast asleep. Bandit puts a bookmark into his book to save his place, and Rascal lies down, and looks around.

He gets back out of bed, and heads to the plate left out for Santa. He crams a piece of General Tso's chicken into his mouth, and goes back to bed.

It's a bitter cold night, and the wind rattles the panes in the window. Kevin softly snores, and it looks like Bandit is asleep, but Rascal has one eye open.

He hears the distant sound of sleigh bells, and whispers, "It must be Santa. I knew Christmas would come. I can't wait."

The door to the clubhouse quietly opens, and there are quiet footsteps and a click, then another quiet footstep and a clump.

"What is this? Where's my milk and cookies! I still don't get any respect. No empty boxes for these raccoons," says an angry voice.

There's someone standing by the Christmas tree dressed in a red coat and a red hat. It can't be Santa. He's too short and he's too thin.

Rascal opens both his eyes and yells, "It's Krampus! It's the Christmas Devil! I told you he was real!"

"It's just Santa Claus, and he's lost weight. He needs more cookies!" exclaims Kevin.

"It's Krampus! Look at his feet!" yells Bandit.

The being dressed as Santa has one black boot on, but the other is a cloven hoof.

"That's right! The fat man in red has been replaced. There's no more Christmas. It's now called Catmas! And cats will rule the world, ha, ha, ha. You raccoons can't stop me!" laughs Krampus.

"You aren't going anywhere. If I can't unravel those Christmas lights, no one can," says Rascal.

"What are you even talking about, you silly raccoon?" replies Krampus.

Krampus looks down and notices that he has stepped into a giant mass of Christmas lights. He reaches down to try to take them off, but he can't. He's stuck.

"I told you the lights go on first," says Kevin.

"Grab the wrapping paper and make sure to secure his arms," says Bandit.

The Totally Ninja Raccoons wrap layer after layer of wrapping paper around Krampus so he can't get free. Rascal ties a bow around one of his horns.

"Now, where's the real Santa Claus?" demands Bandit.

"I'll never tell," says Krampus.

"We will rescue Santa and save Christmas," says Bandit.

"Okay, but can we do it tomorrow, after a long winter's nap?" yawns Kevin.

"Come on, we're raccoons. We are nocturnal, after all," replies Bandit.

"You ninny raccoons will never ever keep me tied up," says Krampus smugly.

There's a puff of smoke, and the smell of a rotten egg. When the smoke clears there is the pile of Christmas lights, untangled. Krampus is gone.

"He's gone!" shouts Rascal.

"Forget about him. I bet I know where Santa is. He's probably locked up in Gypsy's secret lair. Let's go! shouts Bandit.

"I get to drive the sleigh!" shouts Kevin.

"Let's just worry about saving Christmas, because we are..."says Bandit.

"The Totally Ninja Raccoons!" shout the three brothers.

Kevin and Bandit start running towards the door.

"Come on, Rascal. Let's go!" shouts Bandit.

"I'm coming," says Rascal. He quickly dashes back to the table and grabs the birch beer.

"I know I shouldn't have put out my last birch beer. Saving Christmas is thirsty work," whispers Rascal.

"Ho, Ho, Ho, what's this? Three raccoons and one traitor?" booms Santa

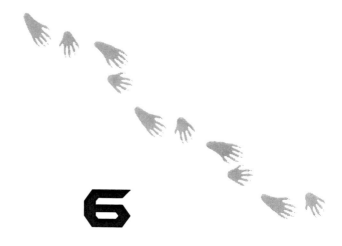

6

WE HAVE A SLEIGH PROBLEM

The Totally Ninja Raccoons dash out into the snow-covered junkyard, and discover Santa's sleigh and reindeer.

"Santa's sleigh!" shouts Kevin.

"And eight HUGE reindeer," says Bandit.

"And my snow cat is ruined! There's a pair of legs where Gypsy's fat head is suppose to be!" shouts Rascal.

"It's Krampus! See the cloven hoof?" yells Bandit.

"Well, he didn't get far," says Kevin.

"Grab a hold of him and pull him out, and don't let him get away this time," says Bandit.

The Ninja Raccoons pull a snow-covered Krampus from what's left of Rascal's snow cat. He's spluttering and is missing his Santa cap.

"Give me back my Santa hat," cries Krampus.

"It's mine now. You ruined my snow cat," says Rascal.

"Your ugly snow cat ruined my escape," spits Krampus.

"You can have the old Santa hat. This one looks better," says Rascal.

"Noooo! I must have that hat, or Gypsy will fire me. I need it to do my Catmas tasks. It's magic. It's how Santa can get inside when there's no chimney."

"We'll be keeping the hat," says Bandit.

"Hey, where's Rudolph?" asks Kevin.

"The forecast calls for it to be cold and clear. So, I left him at the North Pole. He doesn't really get along with the other reindeer," answered Krampus.

"We should borrow the sleigh to rescue Santa Claus," says Kevin.

"I'll drive!" says Rascal.

"Ha, you might have discovered one part of Santa's magic, but you'll never figure out the sled, and I'll never tell you what it is," says Krampus.

"We'll just ask Santa. I bet he's at Gypsy's super-secret hideout," says Rascal.

"Except it's not so secret anymore," says Kevin.

"We know right where it is," says Bandit.

"I have a map!" chirps Rascal.

The Totally Ninja Raccoons tie up Krampus and put him on the sled, and pull him along to Gypsy's formerly super-secret lair.

"Here we are, and it looks like no one is guarding the place," says Bandit.

"Gypsy is probably sleeping with visions of sugar plums dancing on her head," says Bandit.

"I could be sleeping. Why would she have sugar-covered plums? Cats don't like sweets," says Kevin.

"A sugar plum is a nut or seed covered in a layer of hard sugar, like those Jordan almonds that Peggy'a Candies has," replies Bandit.

"I love those. Soooo crunchy, sooo delicious," says Rascal.

"Next you are going to tell me that those bear paws aren't made form real bears, but just another type of doughnut," says Kevin.

"I love doughnuts," says Rascal.

"We know!" shout Kevin and Bandit.

"It's time to focus, ninjas. We need to rescue Santa and save Christmas for all the boys and girls," says Bandit.

The Totally Ninja Raccoons quietly enter the cave, dragging Krampus behind them. It's damp and musty. A lone light bulb shines on the big, metal cage that Bigfoot was supposed to occupy. There is Santa Claus.

"Ho, Ho, Ho, what's this? Three raccoons and one traitor?" booms Santa.

The three brothers answer at the same time, "We are the Totally Ninja Raccoons and we are here to rescue you and save Christmas."

"We captured the impostor, Krampus, and brought him here to be locked up," says Bandit.

"I just wanted to drive the sleigh and deliver fun for a change. Why do I always have to be the bad guy?" whines Krampus.

"I want to drive the sleigh!' shouts Rascal.

"I'm the only one that can drive the sleigh now that Krampus is caught, and there won't be any Christmas to save if you don't get me out of this cage!" says Santa.

"We'll get you out of there!" shout the Ninja Raccoons.

"Rascal, get Santa out of that cage!" says Bandit.

"Right away, Santa, sir," replies Rascal.

Rascal takes out his rusty, but trusty, screwdriver. He holds it up to the lock.

"This screwdriver is too big, and I left my smaller ones back at the clubhouse," says Rascal.

From the entrance of the cave comes a soft meow and a voice, "I want to drive the sleigh. I love Christmas."

"Can you get me out of this cage?" asks Santa.

Huck holds up his paw, and pops out a claw shaped like a key.

"I'm Huck, and I can open anything with these," smirks Huck.

Huck unlocks the cage, and Santa hurries out. The ninja Raccoons get ready to throw Krampus in when Krampus starts crying.

"No! Wait! I just want to deliver presents," cries Krampus.

Santa strokes his big, white bearded chin and checks his pocket watch, "I am behind schedule and am going to need all the help I can get."

"We'll help! We could get our friend, the Thunderbird, and deliver presents!" say the Ninja Raccoons together.

"I get to drive Santa's sleigh!" yells Huck.

"You need to Santa's magic to do that," says Rascal.

"Nah, you just need the keys. They are in my right pocket. I'll give them to you if you just untie me," says Krampus.

"I'll take Krampus and Huck, and you Ninja Raccoons take my extra bag and deliver presents to all of Tioga County and we should just be able to make it," says Santa.

"Let's do this because we are..." says Bandit.

"The Totally Ninja--" shout Rascal, Bandit and Kevin.

"Cats?" meows Huck.

"Raccoons!" shout the Totally Ninja Raccoons.

"Let's save Christmas!" shouts Santa.

Everyone rushes out of the cave. Rascal runs back in, and leaves a beautifully-wrapped gift on Gypsy's desk.

"Noooo! It's coal," cries Gypsy

7

GYPSY'S SURPRISE

It's Christmas morning in Wellsboro, and Gypsy is up early, for Gypsy. She slowly makes her way down the steps, yawns, and does a lazy cat stretch.

"That was a long winter's nap. Now, it's time to make Santa give me my Catmas present," says Gypsy.

Gypsy waddles over to the big, iron cage.

"Wakey, wakey, Santa. What did you gift me? Oh, that's right. You were in the cold cage all night," meows Gypsy.

Gypsy goes over and knocks on the bars. The blanket-covered lump on the bed isn't moving. She reaches through the bars and pokes it, but Santa still doesn't move.

Gypsy opens the doors and pulls off the blanket only to find a pillow!

"Santa is gone! It must be those pesky Ninja Raccoons. Catmas is ruined!" yowls Gypsy.

Gypsy looks around the cave and sees a beautifully-wrapped gift on her desk.

"Well, maybe not completely ruined. It looks like Santa left me a present anyway," meows Gypsy.

Gypsy pops out her claws, cuts the tape, and unwraps the present. Poof! A large cloud of smoke rolls out, filling the cave.

"Pee-Yoo, it's a stink bomb! Those darn raccoons. Wait, there's something in there," says Gypsy.

Gypsy peers into the bottom of the box to find something black and hard.

"Noooo! It's coal," cries Gypsy.

41

"Totally!" Shout the three Ninja Raccoons

8

MEANING OF CHRISTMAS

It's dawn, and the sun is just beginning to come up over the mountains. The Thunderbird lands with a thump in the junkyard, and the Ninja Raccoons climb down.

"That was a lot of fun, helping deliver those presents!" says Kevin.

"I really wanted to drive Santa's sled," says Rascal.

"That would have been super-cool, but it was nice that the Thunderbird was available to help us out on Christmas Eve," says Kevin.

"Yeah, you'd think he'd be decorating his tree for Christmas," says Rascal.

"Not everyone celebrates Christmas," explains Bandit.

"Speaking of Christmas, we were so busy rescuing Santa and saving Christmas..." says Kevin.

"That Santa never made it to our house," says Rascal, sounding disappointed.

"That's okay. The true meaning of the season is giving, and we helped Santa give to the rest of the world," says Bandit.

"There's always next year, I guess," says Kevin.

The Ninja Raccoons take off their Santa hats and walk into the clubhouse. There they find a Christmas tree strung with light bulbs, and tinsel. There are many presents under the tree.

"It looks like Christmas came after all!" yells Rascal.

"Totally! shout the three Ninja Raccoons.

THE END

About Krampus

What is a Krampus? Krampus is a creature from Germanic myth. His name comes from the German word "krampen" which means "claw."

He is described as being half-goat and half-man and hairy all over. He wears a chain and carries a bundle of birch sticks to hit naughty children.

He arrives before Santa Claus on a night all his own. He shows up on Krampus Night, or Krampusnacht. Children leave their shoes out, and if they find a gift, they have been good, but if they find a birch rod, they've been naughty.

Some say Krampus is misunderstood and that he works alongside Santa to ensure good prevails. Some tales says he drags naughty children away, never to be seen again. Is Krampus real? Become a reading ninja and decide for yourself.

About the Author

Kevin resides in Wellsboro, just a short hike from the Pennsylvania Grand Canyon. When he's not writing, you can find him at *From My Shelf Books & Gifts*, an independent bookstore he runs with his lovely wife, several helpful employees, and two friendly cats, Huck & Finn.

He's recently become an honorary member of the Cat Board, and when he's not scooping the litter box, or feeding Gypsy her tuna, he's writing more stories about the Totally Ninja Raccoons. Be sure to catch their next big adventure, *The Totally Ninja Raccoons and the Secret of Nessmuk Lake*.

You can write him at:

From My Shelf Books & Gifts
7 East Ave., Suite 101
Wellsboro, PA 16901

www.wellsborobookstore.com

About the Illustrator

Jubal Lee is a former Wellsboro resident who now resides in sunny Florida, due to his extreme allergic reaction to cold weather.

He is an eclectic artist who, when not drawing raccoons, werewolves, and the like, enjoys writing, bicycling, and short walks on the beach.